My Book of Favourite
Fairy Stories

HAMLYN

CONTENTS

Cover illustration by Peter Dennis

Cover design by Kasa and Steel

Published 1987 by Hamlyn Publishing
a division of The Hamlyn Publishing Group Limited
Bridge House, London Road,
Twickenham, Middlesex, England

All the material in this compilation was originally published in *Storyteller*.

Copyright © Marshall Cavendish Limited 1982, 1983, 1984
This edition © Marshall Cavendish Limited 1987

Produced by Marshall Cavendish Limited

ISBN 0 600 53106 6

Printed and bound in Vicenza, Italy by L.E.G.O.

DICK WHITTINGTON and his CAT

Dick Whittington woke one morning with a handkering for adventure. He bounded out of the house and on to the village green.

"Hey!" an old farmer called to the boy, "you ought to take yourself off to London. It's too quiet round here for the likes of you. They do say that the streets there be paved with gold."

Dick was amazed. "Gold! Then just one cobblestone would make me rich!"

"But then again, I never believe what town folk say," added the farmer, laughing.

But he was too late to stop Dick. The young man had two words ringing in his ears: 'London' and 'gold'. "And now to the city," he cried, "to make my fortune!"

The first signpost outside the village said 'London'. "Good," thought Dick, "it must be just over the hill." But London was not just over the hill; nor over the next, nor the next. Exhausted, Dick lay down to sleep in the shelter of an old oak tree.

In the middle of the night he was awakened by a tickling on his cheek. Sitting up, he saw a marmalade cat smiling at him. "Excuse me, sir," said the cat, "but have you got a saucer of milk to spare?"

"I'm sorry," said Dick. "All the food and drink I set off with has gone, and I've no money to buy more·"

"Never mind," said the cat. "If we curl up together at least we'll be warm."

3

And there it lay, round the next corner, the gleaming, smoking, ramshackle chaos of London. The roads were suddenly busy. Everybody seemed to be shouting and hurrying, pushing and quarrelling. But the streets were not paved with gold — they were running with mud.

Dick and Tom ducked out of the way of the thronging crowds, and ran through an arch and into a courtyard. Dick knocked on the basement door of a grand-looking house. "Er, have you got a job for a hard-working country boy?" he shouted.

A fearsome face as white as dough

And that is how Dick made friends with his cat, who very soon told him that his name was Tom. In the morning they travelled on together towards London. On and on they walked until at last Dick said, "I'm going back, Tom. I've had enough. There can't be anything in London that's worth all this walking." And he turned his back on London and began trudging home.

At that very moment the sound of bells began to ring across the fields. They were the church bells of the City of London and they seemed to be singing:

"Turn again Whittington,
Lord Mayor of London!"

Over and over again they chimed, until the words jangled in Dick's head.

"You can't give up now!" cried Tom. "Onwards to London!"

and crowned with fiery red hair appeared round the door. "Come in 'ere, boy, and scrape the pots. I'm cook in this house. If you work hard, I might let you eat the scrapings!"

And that was how Dick came to work in the house of Captain Fitzwarren. He worked so hard scraping and polishing that by evening he wanted only to sleep. But the mice that infested his attic bedroom kept him awake — until one night he said to Tom, "Go get 'em, boy!" And the mice ran for their lives. Dick's cat was a great comfort to him.

So, too, was Captain Fitzwarren's young daughter, Alice. She would often come down the to the kitchen to sit and talk with Dick. And she loved to stroke

Tom as he lay by the fire.

"If I were Lord Mayor of London" Dick used to say laughingly, "I'd marry you, Alice Fitzwarren." And Alice would smile and say, "If you did become Lord Mayor of London, of course I'd marry you." And the cat would purr and say, "Who knows? Who knows?"

One day, Captain Fitzwarren announced that he was setting sail on a voyage. He gathered together his family and servants, and said goodbye to them all. When he noticed Dick standing beside the cook, his cat in his arms, he said, "Now that's just what I need. Here's a silver shilling, boy, for your cat. He's a ship's cat now." Dick tried to protest, but the cook smacked him sharply. "Do as you're told, and don't argue with the master!" Dick returned sadly to his chilly attic, but it was so lonely without Tom that he decided to go and fetch him back. Just before dawn, he crept up the gangplank of the ship, little knowing that it was just about to sail.

And *that* is how Dick came to be cabin boy aboard Captain Fitzwarren's ship, and to sail to the mysterious lands of the East.

After weeks in storm-tossed waters, the ship ran aground on a strange, uncharted shore. Strange, warlike soldiers escorted the ship's company to the Sultan Suleiman's palace — cargo, cat and all.

"Mighty Suleiman!" said Fitzwarren spreading the entire ship's cargo before him, "I bring a few humble possessions in the hope of pleasing your eminence."

"Hmm," said the Sultan. "I have every possession a man could desire. What need have I of these trinkets?"

As the Sultan spoke, Dick could not help but notice that the whole palace was overrun with mice and rats. Tom wriggled restlessly in Dick's arms. "Rrrow! rrow! I can't bear it another minute!"

Leaping out of Dick's arms, he pounced towards the Sultan's daughter, the Sultana, dived under her throne, and came out dragging a huge rat in his jaws! "O Sun and Moon!" shrieked the Sultana.

"What wonderful beast is this?" Tom ran round the palace, scattering mice and rats, and swallowing a dozen or more. "O marvellous beast!" cried the Sultan. "During my reign and the reign of my father, this country has been plagued with rats. But this creature is a veritable slayer of rats! Name your price, Captain! For this creature I will pay a sack of diamonds!"

Dick caught Tom up in his arms. "Oh, but he's my friend, sir. I couldn't leave him behind in a foreign land!" The cat whispered in Dick's ear. Dick set him down on the floor and he ran towards the ship. "He will return," said Dick. Impatiently the Sultan waited. Anxiously Dick and the Captain watched the door for the cat's return. At last a small, whiskered face peeped round the door, and Tom returned — leading a family of kittens! At once they began pouncing on mice.

"You have always had cats in your country," said Tom. "But they were frightened by your warlike ways. These six would be most proud and honoured to serve you and your son, and your son's sons — as long as you put away your swords. And now, if it please your Excellency, I'd like to go home with my friend Dick."

The Sultan clapped his hands with delight. "O Earth and Sky! but this is wonderful! I have six rat-slayers instead of one! Great must be the reward for those who brought me these cat-beasts! To the boy Dick I offer my daughter — yes, my own daughter — for a wife. You aren't married, are you boy?"

Dick bowed very low. "No, your Gloriousness, but I have sworn to marry none other than the beautiful Alice Fitzwarren, daughter of this worthy sea-captain." The Sultan was disappointed, and the Sultana was *very* disappointed. But they comforted themselves by giving Dick three sacks of diamonds and a turban.

"O most generous Suleiman!" said Dick. "Our boat is grounded on your beautiful shores, and without help we can never return home."

"Not another word!" cried

8

the Sultan. "Here are two flying carpets woven by my own magician — one for the ship's crew and another for my humble gift of treasure."

And *that* is how Dick Whittington came to London. As the two carpets swooped over the roof of the house, Alice looked out of her window and waved.

"Dick!" cried the captain, climbing off the carpet, "now that you've made your fortune, you're as good a husband as I could wish for my Alice. And what's more, I do believe she's in love with you. Why not run and ask her?"

"Do you remember my promise?" said Alice. "I vowed to marry you if ever you became Lord Mayor of London."

Such was his love for Alice that Dick immediately set to work. Using the treasure given him by the Sultan he soon became a rich and successful merchant. He was hard-working, popular and fair; and before two years had passed he was elected Lord Mayor of London.

On the day of the wedding the streets were filled with people, all agog to see the new Lord Mayor and his beautiful bride.

Tom sat beside Dick and Alice in their golden coach, wearing a new ribbon with a bright silver bell.

But no-one could hear it ringing above the huge pealing chimes of the bells of the City of London, as they rang out:
"Hail Richard Whittington
Lord Mayor of London."

The Snow Queen

Once, long ago, there was a little boy called Kai and a little girl called Gerda. They lived next door to each other, and they loved each other very much.

Between their two houses was a garden where Kai and Gerda played among the flowers all summer long. Gerda's favourite flowers were the roses, and she made up a verse about them, specially for Kai:

"*Until the last rose blooms and dies,*
We will be friends, Gerda and Kai."

When winter came, they sat inside by the warm stove and listened to Kai's grandmother telling stories about the wicked Snow Queen.

"She flies with the sleet and smothers the fields with snow. She stiffens the flowers with frost and freezes the rivers. Her heart is a block of ice. And she would like to make everyone's heart icy."

As the old woman spoke, the wind howled round the house, and a window clattered open. A flurry of sleet blew into Kai's face, and a splinter of ice pierced his eye. Instantly, it travelled to his heart and lodged there.

Kai cried out in pain. But a few moments later he was laughing again.

The next day, Kai went to play in the town square with the other boys.

"Can I come?" said Gerda.

But Kai turned on her angrily. "Of course not. You're only a stupid girl."

Gerda was very hurt. How could she know that the icicle in Kai's heart was turning it to ice?

The boys liked to tie their sledges to the farmer's cart, which pulled them across the snow. But this day a big white sleigh stood in the square, its driver dressed in white fur.

"This will be better than the farmer's cart," thought Kai, and he tied his sledge to the back of the white sleigh.

The sleigh moved off — faster and faster, until Kai began to get frightened. He wanted to untie his sledge, but could not undo the rope. On and on they went, out of the city gates, on and on, flying with the wind.

"Help! Help!" shouted Kai, but nobody heard him. They flew for hours, until suddenly they stopped and the driver stood up. The driver was a tall, thin woman and her coat and hat were made of snow. Kai stared in wonder. There before him stood the Snow Queen!

She lifted Kai into the sleigh beside her and wrapped him in her coat. "You're cold," she said, and kissed him on the forehead. Though her kiss was like ice, Kai no longer felt the cold. He thought that nobody in the world could be more

boat will carry me to Kai," she thought.

The boat carried Gerda down the river until it passed a little thatched house beside a cherry orchard. A strange old lady came out of the cottage wearing a large hat. With her crooked walking stick, she hooked the boat and pulled it to the shore.

beautiful than the Snow Queen. For it was she who had sent the wind to plunge an icicle into Kai's heart. By now, it had turned to solid ice. And he forgot all about Gerda and his grandmother.

Gerda wept bitterly when Kai did not come home. Everyone said he must be dead, lost somewhere in the deep snow. All winter she waited, but Kai did not come back. At last the warmer weather came. And Gerda was given new red shoes to wear with her Spring clothes.

She put them on and went to the wide river. "Have you seen my friend Kai?" she asked the waves. "I'll give you my new red shoes if you tell me where he is!"

The tumbling waves nodded their foaming heads. So she climbed into a little boat moored among the reeds, then tossed her shoes as far as she could into the water. As she did so, the boat drifted away from the bank and began racing downstream. Gerda was frightened, but she dared not jump out. "Perhaps the

Now in truth, the old lady was the loneliest of all magicians, and she wanted to keep Gerda with her. So she combed away all her memories. Soon Gerda forgot all about Kai.

For days Gerda played in the cottage. But one sunny morning she was wandering among the flowers in the garden when she saw a bush blossoming with red roses. Gerda kissed the flowers in delight, and straight away she remembered Kai.

"I've stayed here too long!" she cried out — and her voice disturbed a big black crow from a nearby tree.

"Caw! What's the matter, little girl?"

"I have to find my friend Kai. Have you seen him?"

"I saw a boy pass this way last week. He had won the heart of a princess, and now he's a prince. They live together in a beautiful palace not far from here."

"Oh, I would be so happy for Kai if he had become a prince," laughed Gerda. "Can you show me the way there?"

So the crow flew off and led little Gerda to the palace. Inside they both

"Poor child," she said to Gerda. "How did you come to be floating all alone through the wide world?"

So Gerda told the old lady her whole story, and asked if she had seen Kai.

"He's not been here yet, my dear, but I expect he will be very soon." She took Gerda into the house and gave her cherries to eat. And while she ate them, the old lady combed the girl's hair.

and faster, and find Kai all the sooner."

In the prince's coach, Gerda rode through a dark forest. The coachwork glistened among the trees — and some wicked robbers saw it, shining in the moonlight.

"It's gold! All gold!" they shouted, and they ambushed it at the next crossroads.

They dragged Gerda out of the the coach and carried her away to their robber castle. At the door stood a black-eyed girl, the daughter of the robber chief.

When they found out that Gerda was not a rich princess and had nothing to steal, they decided to kill her. "Oh don't do that!" cried the robber's daughter. "She can play with me, and I can wear her pretty clothes!"

crept up a shadowy staircase until they came to the royal bedchamber. Gerda peeped in at the sleeping prince — and burst into tears.

"Oh, Crow! It isn't Kai at all! I'll have to go on looking. But I'm so tired!"

Her crying woke the young prince and princess, and they were amazed to see a little girl sobbing at the foot of their bed. But when they heard her story, they understood her tears.

"I'll give you my prettiest dress to cheer you up," said the princess.

"And I'll give you my golden coach," said the prince, "so you can travel farther

snow, and the Queen has a summer palace there."

"I must get there quickly!" exclaimed Gerda. "Now I understand why he was unkind to me that day. His heart was turning to ice!"

The robbers were sleeping. The chief's daughter crept to her father's pillow and stole the key to set Gerda free. "Take her to Lapland," she told the reindeer. "Help her to find Kai."

The reindeer was delighted to be going home, and he leapt over the moors and marshes. They travelled for several days and nights, until at last they came to Lapland. It was very, very cold, with ice and snow everywhere.

The robber chief scowled. "All right, then. But I'll keep her under lock and key, or she might escape and give away our hiding place."

That night, Gerda told her new friend about Kai, and how she longed to find him. As she spoke, the doves in the rafters and an old reindeer listened to her story.

Suddenly one of the doves said, "Coo, coo. We've seen little Kai. He rode in the Snow Queen's sleigh as she flew towards Lapland."

"Ah yes," said the reindeer. "I was born in Lapland. It glitters with ice and

remembered her.

"Gerda! It's you!" he laughed. And they hugged and kissed each other and danced for joy. The pieces of ice danced too, and shaped the word ETERNITY on the icy floor. "Now I'm free!" cried Kai. "I'm free of the Snow Queen's powers.

Gerda led Kai to the palace where the reindeer was waiting. As they travelled back, the sun shone brightly, and by the time they reached home, it was Summer again. And the roses in the garden were in full bloom.

"Look! Over there!" cried Gerda. Sparkling in the distance was the Snow Queen's summer palace.

Inside her palace, the Snow Queen had made Kai her slave. She was as sharp-tongued and spiteful as frost, forcing him to polish the vast, icy floors. He would have wept, but his heart was too frozen for tears.

The Snow Queen gave Kai some icicles and said, "Shape these into the word ETERNITY, and I *may* set you free." Then she flew away to heap snow on the cities and fetch down avalanches on the heads of climbers. Kai was left alone with the icicles. His hands were blue with cold, but he felt nothing. He was still trying to shape the word ETERNITY when Gerda found her way into the palace and to his frozen room.

"Kai!" she cried. "I've found you at last!" And she flung her arms around him.

But Kai stood still and cold and unsmiling. "Who are you? What are you doing here? Are you another of the Snow Queen's slaves? Go away. Let go of me!"

Gerda refused to let go. Despite his unkind looks, she wept tears of happiness at seeing him again. And as she cried, her warm tears trickled into Kai's eye . . . and melted the ice in his heart. And Kai

maid, gold and jewels . . . Well, I was so busy making the list that I didn't have time to make dinner!"

"What!" snapped Cedric. "No dinner? How am I expected to make important decisions on an empty stomach? It's not much to ask is it? You're so lazy, Magda. I do wish there had been something cooked and waiting — even if it was just a few sausages."

THE THREE WISHES

When Cedric got home one evening, sour and grumpy as usual, his wife was sitting in the kitchen chair with a very strange look on her face. Crumpled in her lap was a letter. "What's the matter with you?" he growled.

"Come in and close the door, Cedric. You won't believe it, but we've had a letter from the fairies. They've granted us *three wishes!*"

He snatched up the letter and slowly read it. "We must make the most of this, Magda. We mustn't be hasty. Three wishes can make us rich — important — famous! But we must ask for the right things."

"I've already made a list," said Magda, jumping up. "Look. A palace for me, a king's crown for you. Beauty for me, long life for you. A queen for a

There was a funny humming noise, like fairy wings and — *Plop!* — a string of sausages appeared on a plate on the kitchen table. Cedric stared at them as they steamed on the plate, and he licked his lips.

"You've wasted a wish!" Magda shouted, beating him over the head with a loaf. "You always were stupid! If a thing needs doing, I have to do it myself, don't I? Cedric Blunder, you make me feel so angry. I . . . I . . . I wish those sausages were hanging on the end of your silly nose!"

There was another small magical sound, like fairies singing and — *Wop!* — the sausages sprang off the plate and stuck to the tip of Cedric's nose. He peered down at them and burst into tears. They both pulled and tugged and tugged and pulled at the dangling sausages.

"Ow, they're so hot!" yelled Cedric.
"Sit still! I'll cut them off."
"Put down that knife, woman!

Oh, how could you?" But the sausages were stuck fast.

Just then, someone knocked at the door. Cedric and Magda stared at each other. "Don't answer it! Do you want all the neighbours to know you've got sausages stuck to your nose?"

"What?" cried Cedric. "Do I have to hide for the rest of my life? Oh, I never realised how lucky I was before, when I had an ordinary nose. If only we weren't so quick to quarrel!"

"Yes, I know, and I'm so very sorry, Cedric."

"No, no, it wasn't your fault, dear. I just wish the fairies had kept their wishes to themselves and left everything as it was."

"So do I."

There was a small sniggering noise, like fairies laughing, and *Blip!* — the sausages dropped off Cedric's nose.

Cedric and Magda hugged each other and laughed and danced round the kitchen. And the fairies at the door ran away to post another letter.

The Selfish Giant

Every afternoon, after school, some children played in the large, beautiful garden of a huge deserted castle. They rolled in the long, soft grass, hid behind the bushes covered with blossom and climbed trees where the birds sang sweetly. They were very happy there.

One afternoon they were playing hide-and-seek when they heard a great voice boom out. "What are you doing in *my* garden?" it roared.

Trembling with fear, the children peered out of their hiding places to see a very angry giant. He had finally decided to come home after living for seven years with his friend, the Cornish ogre. "I came back to my castle for some peace and quiet," he thundered. "I don't want to listen to a lot of children laughing and shouting. Get out of my garden — and don't come back."

So the children ran away, as fast as their legs would carry them.

"This garden belongs to me, and nobody else," the giant mumbled to himself. "I shall make sure that nobody else can use it." So he built a high wall all around it, with sharp iron spikes on top.

In the wall was a great iron gate, and

on the gate the giant put a notice. 'KEEP OUT', it read. 'TRESPASSERS WILL BE PROSECUTED'. Every day the children poked their noses through the bars of the gate and looked longingly at the garden. Then, sadly, they wandered off to play on the hard, dusty road.

KEEP
OUT!
Trespassers
will be
prosecuted

Soon the Winter came. Snow covered the ground with a thick white mantle and Frost painted the trees silver. The North Wind howled round the giant's castle and Hail pounded the window-panes. "How I long for the Spring," the giant sighed, as he sat huddled by the fire.

At last Spring came. The Snow and the Frost disappeared and the flowers pushed their heads up through the ground. The buds on the trees opened and the birds sang merrily — except in the giant's garden. There the Snow, the Frost, and the North Wind still danced through the bare branches of the trees. "The Spring has refused to come to this garden," they cried. "At last we have a place where we can stay for ever."

One morning the giant was lying
awake in bed, feeling very sorry for
himself, when he heard a blackbird
singing. He leapt over to the window
and beamed with pleasure. The Snow
and the Frost had gone, and every tree
had burst into blossom.

Every tree also held one of the
children whom the giant had frightened
away. They had crept into the garden
through a hole in the wall, and the Spring
had rushed in after them. Only one child
was still standing on the ground. He was a
boy who was crying bitterly because he
was too small to reach even the lowest
branch of the smallest tree.

The giant was moved to pity. "How
selfish I have been," he said to himself.
"Now I see why the Spring wouldn't
come to my garden. I'll knock down the

walls and turn it into a children's
playground. But first I'll put that poor little
boy on top of a tree."

The giant crept down the stairs and
into the garden, but when the children
saw him they were so frightened they ran
away again. Only the little boy, whose
eyes were so full of tears that he could not
see the giant coming, stayed where he
was. As the Winter returned to the
garden, the giant gently picked up the
boy. "There's no need to cry," he
murmured softly, and he placed the boy
on top of the nearest tree. Immediately

the tree burst into blossom. And the boy flung his arms round the giant's neck and kissed him.

When the children saw that the giant was kind and friendly, they came running back into the garden through the hole in the wall, followed by the Spring. The giant laughed happily and joined in their games, only stopping to knock down the walls with an axe. It was sunset before he realised that he had not seen the small boy for some time.

"Where is your little friend?" he asked anxiously. But the children did not know.

Every day after school the children came to play in the giant's beautiful garden. Every day the giant asked them the same question: "Is the little boy with you today?" And every day the answer was the same:

"We don't know where to find him. The only time we've ever seen him was the day you knocked down the wall."

The giant felt sad because he loved the little boy very much. Only the sight of the children playing made him happy again.

on your hands and feet? Old and feeble as I am, I'll kill the people who have done this to you."

Then the child smiled gently and said, "Hush. Don't be angry, but come with me."

"Who are you?" whispered the giant, falling to his knees.

"A long time ago you let me play in your garden," the child replied. "Now I want you to come and play in mine. It's called Paradise."

That afternoon, when the children ran into the garden to play in the snow, they found the dead giant lying peacefully under a tree, all covered with blossom.

The years passed quickly and the giant grew old and weak. Soon he could no longer play with all the children.

One winter morning he was sitting by his bedroom window when he suddenly saw the most beautiful tree he had ever seen, standing in a corner of the garden. Its golden branches were covered with delicate white blossom and silver fruit — and underneath them stood the little boy.

"He's come back at last," the giant said joyfully. Forgetting how weak his legs were, he rushed down the stairs and hurried across the garden. But as he reached the little boy his face became red with anger. "Who has hurt you?" he cried. "Why can I see the marks of nails

Rapunzel

Long, long ago, in a wild and dangerous land, there lived a good man and his wife. They longed to have a child and waited patiently, year after year. Then, at last, the woman found that she was expecting a baby.

Now the couple lived next door to a beautiful garden which was surrounded by a high wall. The garden belonged to a fierce witch, and nobody had ever dared go in, for fear the witch would cast a wicked spell on them. At the back of the couple's house a little window over-looked the garden. The woman often stood there, gazing down at the wonderful things the witch had grown — flowers, trees and herbs with magic powers.

One day the woman fell ill. She had to stay in bed, and lost her appetite.

Every day her husband brought her good things to eat, but she would not touch any of them. "Please," he begged her, "tell me what I can bring. There must be something that will cure you."

"Bring me a sprig of the rapunzel herb that grows in the witch's garden," she whispered. "That will make me well again."

The husband was very frightened, but he was ready to do anything to help his wife get better. "The old witch won't harm me," he told himself. He waited until nightfall, then he climbed over the wall into the witch's garden. With a pounding heart, he looked around him. Nobody was there. He quickly found some rapunzel, snatched a sprig of it, and hurried home.

snapped the witch, "but on one condition. In return for the rapunzel, you must give me your first-born child."

The husband was so desperate that he agreed, and rushed back to his wife.

A few months later, the couple had a baby daughter. And on the very day she was born, the witch appeared. The couple begged her to let them keep the child, but the witch took no notice of them.

"I'll call the girl Rapunzel," she laughed cruelly. And she swept the baby up into her cloak and carried her away.

Rapunzel grew up to be a very beautiful girl. She had eyes the colour of violets and long, long hair as fine as spun gold, which she wore in a thick plait. When Rapunzel was twelve, the witch took her deep into a dark, gloomy forest and locked her up in a tall tower. It had no door and no stairs — just one tiny window in the chamber at the very top.

Rapunzel was shut away from the world. It forgot her. The only person she ever saw was the old witch, who visited her every day with food. She stood at the

His wife felt much better when she had eaten the herb. But the next day she wanted some more. "Please," she begged her husband, "if you don't bring more rapunzel, I'll die."

So late that night, her husband climbed back over the wall into the witch's garden. Just as he was pulling up the herb, the witch suddenly appeared.

"Thief!" she screeched. "A curse on you! How dare you come into my garden and steal my plants!"

"Oh, please!" begged the man. "My wife is very ill and she'll die if she doesn't have this herb."

"Very well, you can have the herb,"

One day, a prince who was riding through the forest lost his way and came past Rapunzel's tower. He heard Rapunzel singing, which she often did so that she would not feel so lonely.

bottom of the tower and called out, "Rapunzel, Rapunzel, let down your hair!"

Then Rapunzel would unwind her plait and throw it down to the witch, who climbed up it as if it were a rope.

The prince had never heard such a pure, sweet voice, and he stopped his horse and strained to listen. He looked for a door to the tower, but could not find one, and he rode away. But the next day he came back, and then every day after that. He was enchanted by the singing and he was determined to find out who was doing the singing.

One day, as the prince stood listening, the witch came. He hid behind a tree and peered out to see what would happen.

"Rapunzel, Rapunzel, let down your hair!" called the witch. Down came Rapunzel's plait and up went the witch into the tower room.

"So that's what I must do to see the singer," thought the prince.

That evening, he went back to the tower. "Rapunzel, Rapunzel, let down your hair!" he called out. There was a soft swishing sound and the golden plait came tumbling down the wall to him. The prince quickly climbed up and scrambled through the window into the tower room.

Rapunzel had never seen a man before. She was very frightened, and backed away. "Who are you?" she gasped.

Don't be afraid," the prince said gently, taking her hands in his. He had fallen in love the very moment he saw her. "I had to find out who was singing so sweetly." And he told her how he had listened every day. Gradually Rapunzel stopped feeling afraid. "Marry me and leave this dreadful prison," he said.

The prince was young and handsome, and Rapunzel liked him. "I'd gladly come with you," she said, "but how shall I ever escape from the tower?

You can climb down my hair, but I have no-one's hair to climb down!" She thought for a moment and then said, "Come and see me every evening, and each time bring me a bundle of silk threads. I'll plait them into a strong rope. When it's finished, we can both climb down and ride away together."

So the prince went to see Rapunzel every evening. And each day she plaited rope with the threads that he brought her. The witch noticed nothing. But Rapunzel was so much in love that she could think of nothing but the prince. One day, as the old woman scrambled over the window-sill, Rapunzel said, without thinking, "Why are you so much heavier to pull up than the prince?"

"You wicked girl!" screeched the witch. "I thought I had locked you up safely. But you've been deceiving me all this time!" She seized an enormous pair of scissors and grabbed hold of Rapunzel's hair. The scissors flashed and

snipped, and the golden plait lay in a coil on the floor. "Now, you ungrateful madam, we'll see how well you do without me!" shrieked the witch. She flew with Rapunzel to a lonely valley, and left her there, all on her own, to live in misery.

Later, as night was falling, the witch went back to the tower to wait for the prince.

After a while, she heard him call: "Rapunzel, Rapunzel, let down your hair." She tied Rapunzel's plait to a heavy chair below the window and threw the golden hair down to the prince. He quickly climbed up, but when he reached the top it was the old witch and not Rapunzel who greeted him at the window.

"She's gone! The girl's gone," cackled the witch. "Your little songbird has flown away and you'll never see her again!" Then she flung the prince down from the tower. He fell into the brambles below, and the sharp thorns scratched his eyes and blinded him. And he staggered away into the forest.

For many years the prince wandered, sad and blind, through forests and mountains. He would have searched for Rapunzel, but how can a man search without eyes? He asked after her, but nobody had seen a beautiful girl with violet eyes and short, golden hair.

Then, one day, he came to a valley. It was a lonely place, but somewhere he could hear sweet singing.

"I know that voice!" he cried. "It's my own love! My Rapunzel!" He followed the sound of her voice, and there, at last, he found her.

The prince was thin and ragged, but Rapunzel recognised him at once. She put her arms round him and wept for joy. As she cried, her warm tears fell on the prince's eyes. In a few seconds, he could see again.

He took Rapunzel back to his kingdom and married her. The marriage was so happy that the news of it spread throughout the world. And when Rapunzel's mother and father heard tell of the beautiful Princess Rapunzel, they knew that their daughter was well and happy, and they were *very* proud.

Clara and the Nutcracker Doll

It was Christmas Eve, and Clara and Franz were waiting for their godfather, Uncle Johann, to arrive. He came to visit them every year to give them their Christmas presents himself. They were very special presents, because Uncle Johann was a toymaker.

"Perhaps he'll come if we shut our eyes and think about him very hard," said Clara.

"Don't be silly," said Franz.

"Oh, let's just try," said Clara. So they both shut their eyes tight and thought very hard.

Just then the doorbell rang. "It worked!" cried Clara, and in came Uncle Johann laughing and shaking the snow off his coat.

"Well, well, well," he cried, hugging them both. "Here you are then. What do you think of these, my little friends?"

He gave Franz and Clara a parcel each. Inside Franz's was a beautiful wooden boat with a bright red sail, and inside Clara's was a doll with very long legs, painted to look like a soldier.

"Who is he?" asked Clara.

"He's a nutcracker doll," said Uncle Johann. "Look." He picked up a nut from a dish on the table, placed it in the doll's mouth, pulled the legs close together and hey presto! The nut's shell cracked open in two neat halves. Uncle Johann popped the nut into Clara's mouth. Clara was thrilled.

"Oh he's lovely, Uncle Johann. I've never had a nutcracker doll before."

And she danced round the room holding her new doll above her head. Her brother Franz had been watching all this time, not saying a word. Suddenly, he dashed across the room, snatched the doll, threw it on the floor and jumped on it. Clara burst into tears. "Oh no! My poor doll!"

Uncle Johann strode across the room, picked up Franz and bundled him out of the door. Clara could hear him speaking very angrily to Franz, as she picked up the nutcracker doll and looked closely at it. She began to smile through her tears. "So, you're not broken after all," she whispered. She curled up on the sofa, with the doll in her arms, and went to sleep.

Later that night, Clara woke to find herself tucked up in her own bed.

"They must have brought me upstairs when I was asleep," she thought. "But where's my nutcracker doll? He must have fallen on the floor again, poor thing."

Quiet as a mouse, Clara put on her slippers and crept downstairs. The clock struck midnight as she opened the door to the drawing room. Startled, she darted across the floor, leaped on to the sofa, and tucked her feet inside her nightdress. She looked all around her.

The fire flared in the grate and lit up the room. Just then there was the sound of stamping feet, and rows of mice came marching by, led by a mouse king with fierce, bright eyes.

Clara's own eyes grew wider and wider as columns of soldiers marched in from the other end of the room. They were Franz's toy soldiers, and leading them all was her nutcracker doll!

The mice and the toy soldiers started to fight. In minutes, the mouse king had driven the nutcracker doll right up against the sofa where Clara was sitting. "Oh no you don't!" she thought.

In a flash, she had taken off a slipper and thrown it at the mouse king. Stunned, he fell to the floor. The nutcracker doll toppled over too and hit his head. The mice rushed forward and carried their king away to safety.

Clara started to pick up the nutcracker doll, but as she did so, quick as a flash, he grew and grew before her very eyes. He was no longer a doll, but a handsome young man. He picked up Clara's slipper, kissed it and gave it back to her.

"Oh yes, please. How do we get there?" Scarcely had she spoken when a boat appeared. Clara and the Prince stepped into it and skimmed off through the wintry night. Snowflakes whirled and danced around them, but Clara felt as warm as if she were wrapped in eiderdown.

At last they arrived at the Nutcracker Prince's palace. Clara gazed at it, entranced. It was made from white icing, with towers of pink icing, columns of barley sugar and chandeliers of glistening pear-drops.

A beautiful, dainty lady welcomed Clara as though she were a princess.

"I am the Sugar Plum Fairy," she said, "and I have all kinds of treats to show you."

"You saved my life. I shall not forget it," he said, smiling at her.

"Who *are* you?" stammered Clara.

"I am the Nutcracker Prince. Will you come with me to my kingdom? It is the Kingdom of Sweets, and no human being has ever visited it before."

"Come with me," said the Prince, and he led Clara into the ballroom, to a peppermint throne studded with silver balls. "Sit here," he said kindly.

"But what is going to happen?"

"All your favourite sweets will dance for you," said the Prince. He smiled and put his finger to his lips as music filled the ballroom.

Clara's heart beat with excitement as two dancers leaped into the middle of the ballroom. They were dressed in rich brown velvet, and Clara watched enthralled as they weaved and stamped to and fro.

"They must be chocolates — my favourite!" she whispered to the Prince. And as if by magic, the dancers became chocolates.

Next came a dozen children, skipping and tripping in candy-coloured dresses.

"Fruit drops!" said Clara, clapping and laughing. "How I love them!"

Then two very tall thin men, dressed in black from head to foot, wobbled to and fro in front of her, in a most comical way.

"Oh, there's no mistaking them! They're Franz's favourite — liquorice!"

In another minute, the Prince had taken Clara's hand and led her on to the dance floor. They whirled around together so fast that the pear-drop chandeliers, the peppermint throne and the walls of white icing all mixed into one bright blur of light.

"Now for the loveliest surprise of all," said the Prince, as he led Clara back to the peppermint throne.

There was a dainty tinkling of music as the Sugar Plum Fairy stepped into the centre of the ballroom. She danced tirelessly, like a snow crystal floating on the wind, and Clara could not take her eyes off her for a second.

"Can she be real?" she wondered, and as she did so she looked down and saw that she was holding her nutcracker doll in her arms.

She blinked, sat up, and looked around. She was once more in her own bed, and the Prince, the ballroom and the Sugar Plum Fairy had all melted away.

"How very strange," thought Clara, and she snuggled down under the covers again, the nutcracker doll under her arm. "I wonder if I will ever see the Kingdom of Sweets again?"

And she fell fast asleep.

The PIED PIPER OF HAMELIN

A rat! A fat, black rat alive with leaping fleas, trailing its long tail through the butter and nibbling the cheese. First one, then two, then ten, then twenty: a plague of rats.

At the start only a handful of houses in Hamelin had a rat: then all the houses in Hamelin had a hundred rats. And every day there were more. First a hundred and then a thousand: then ten thousand and then . . . a million rats.

The people of Hamelin tried everything to be rid of the rats. They chased them with sticks, threw water over them by the bucketful, and baited traps with poisoned cheese. But for every ten rats they killed, they seemed to be twenty more. First the people drove the rats out of their houses. Then the rats drove the people out of their houses — and soon everyone was gathered in the town square, in front of the Mayor's house.

"Get rid of the rats!" they shouted "You're the Mayor — get rid of the rats!"

The Mayor came out of his large house, shaking a big black rat off the hem of his robe. "What's everybody doing here? Clear the square!"

"What are you doing about the rats?" they demanded.

"Um, well, er . . . I'm thinking about it," said the Mayor.

"It's not good enough!" the people shouted. "Get rid of the rats, or we'll get rid of you!"

Suddenly, a clear voice rang out above all the shouting. It silenced everyone, even the Mayor. "*I* will get rid of the rats."

The crowd parted. A stranger walked towards the Mayor — tall and thin and upright, dressed in strange colourful clothes. His jerkin was a vivid green, with studs and buckles and gold embroidery. His waistcoat was a rich, cherry red to match the long, trailing feather in his hatband. And his orange leggings were striped with emerald green. His eyes were a piercing, animal yellow, and a long moustache hung from his top lip like two limp rats' tails.

"You can get rid of the rats?" asked somebody in the crowd.

"I can. They'll leave if I tell them, and never come back."

"Well, do it, man!" urged the mayor.

"I shall want paying," said the stranger from between his thin lips. "A shilling a rat." The news swept through the crowd in whispers. "A shilling a rat! He wants a shilling a rat!"

"A shilling a head?" screeched the Mayor. "Do you think we're made of money? Do you know how many rats we have here in Hamelin?"

"I've made a rough count," said the stranger. "About a million."

"You must give us time to think about it," said the Mayor. "I shall go and consult the town council. It's an awful lot of money."

"There are an awful lot of rats," said the stranger, and he almost smiled.

"The council will want to know who they are dealing with. What name shall I tell them?"

send him packing without a penny!"

"That's the answer," cried the town clerk. "What a plan! No wonder you're the Mayor!"

The Pied Piper was still sitting on the fountain wall when the Mayor came out of the town hall. "Well? Have you made up your minds?"

"We have indeed, young man," said the mayor. "We'll gladly pay you a shilling a head if you get rid of all of them and they don't come back again. You have our solemn word on it. When can you start?"

"I'll do it tonight," said the Pied Piper. "Tell everybody to stay indoors."

The Mayor smiled generously, gathered up his robes and walked in a mayor-like way back to his house. His five children met him on the steps

"People call me the Pied Piper," the stranger replied. "You have until sunset to decide. I'll wait here until then." And he sat down on the edge of the fountain in the square. Opening the leather bag, he took out a brass pipe. There he sat, cleaning the pipe with a piece of rag, as the midday sun passed overhead. The Mayor scurried over to the town hall, straightening his chain of office.

"There's a man out there who says he can get rid of the rats. In fact he looks a bit like a rat himself. Funny eyes."

"What's he charging?" the councillors asked. "Can we afford him?"

"He wants a shilling a head."

"A shilling a head! What a price! We'll have to put up the rates and the people won't like that. They may not like rats, but they hate parting with their money!"

"Who said anything about paying?" The Mayor grinned. "Why not agree to his price and let him get rid of the rats. When they are gone and he asks for his money, we can

in tears: "The rats have eaten the dinner, Daddy, and bitten the baby. What are you doing about them?"

"There's nothing to worry about, children," he said. "Tomorrow, there won't be a rat left in Hamelin and we'll be able to sleep peacefully in our beds. It was the smartest thing this town ever did when it made me the Mayor!"

When the sun had gone down, and the people of Hamelin were at home in their rat-infested houses, a lonely figure appeared in the town square. The Pied Piper, his brass flute in his hand, stood looking at the rising moon.

He put the flute to his lips and began to play — a sad, haunting melody, a tune unknown to any of the citizens of Hamelin as they listened in their lighted windows. Such a lot of music from such a small pipe! It floated across the square and into every alley, it echoed in every doorway, it drifted over every rooftop. Nobody in Hamelin could escape hearing it. Nor could the rats.

Something moved in the darkness. It was a fat, black rat sitting back on its haunches, its head to one side, listening. The shadows seethed with rats.

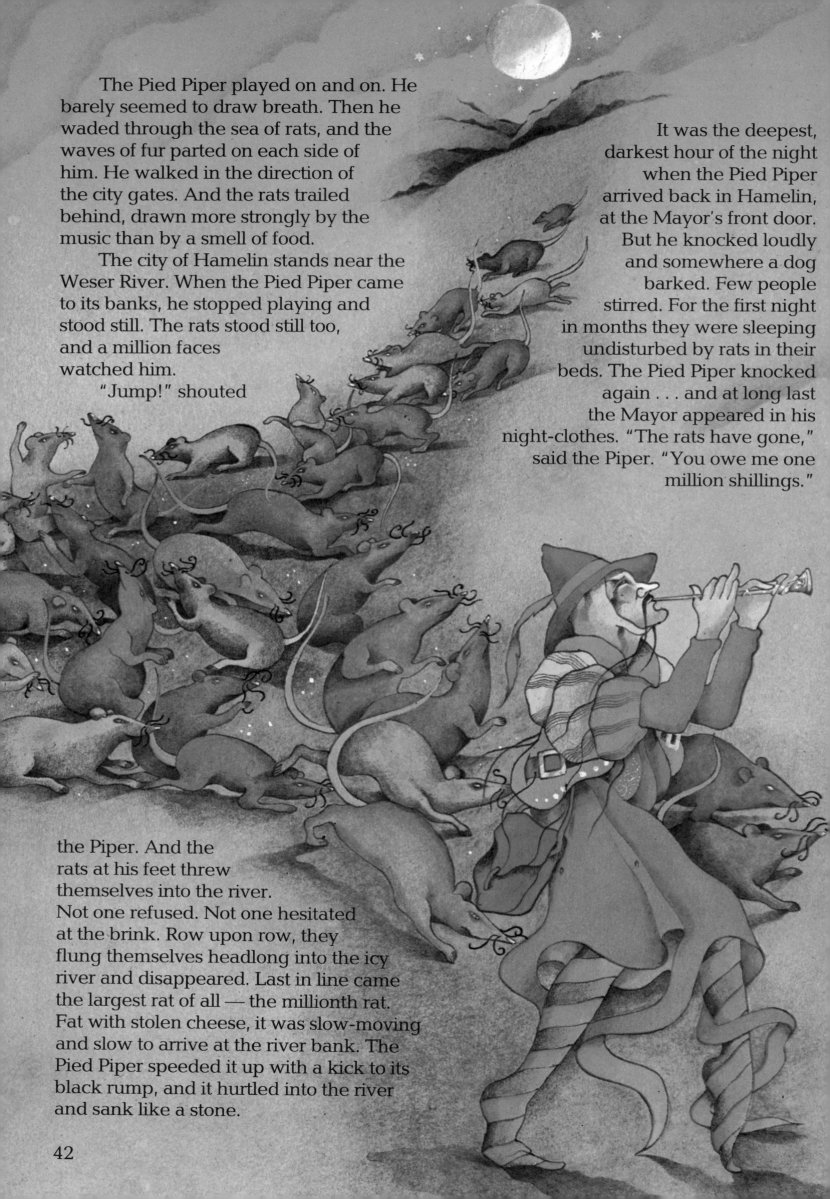

The Pied Piper played on and on. He barely seemed to draw breath. Then he waded through the sea of rats, and the waves of fur parted on each side of him. He walked in the direction of the city gates. And the rats trailed behind, drawn more strongly by the music than by a smell of food.

The city of Hamelin stands near the Weser River. When the Pied Piper came to its banks, he stopped playing and stood still. The rats stood still too, and a million faces watched him.

"Jump!" shouted

It was the deepest, darkest hour of the night when the Pied Piper arrived back in Hamelin, at the Mayor's front door. But he knocked loudly and somewhere a dog barked. Few people stirred. For the first night in months they were sleeping undisturbed by rats in their beds. The Pied Piper knocked again . . . and at long last the Mayor appeared in his night-clothes. "The rats have gone," said the Piper. "You owe me one million shillings."

the Piper. And the rats at his feet threw themselves into the river. Not one refused. Not one hesitated at the brink. Row upon row, they flung themselves headlong into the icy river and disappeared. Last in line came the largest rat of all — the millionth rat. Fat with stolen cheese, it was slow-moving and slow to arrive at the river bank. The Pied Piper speeded it up with a kick to its black rump, and it hurtled into the river and sank like a stone.

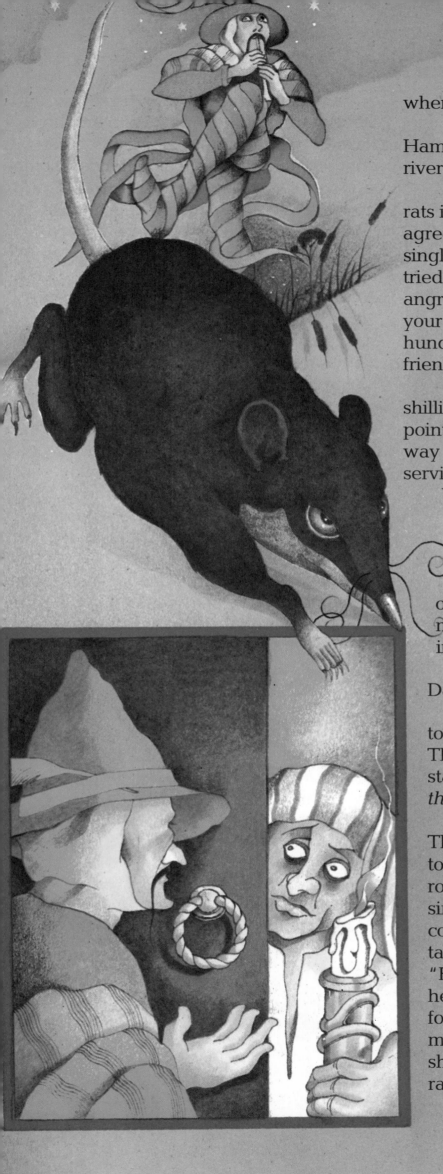

"Gone? One million of them? Well, where's your proof? Where are they?"

"You wanted them gone from Hamelin. The rats are all drowned in the river and I claim my shilling a rat."

"Nonsense. I'm not going to pay for rats in a river! A shilling a head, we agreed — and you haven't brought me a single head! Now be off with you!" He tried to slam the door: The Pied Piper's angry yellow eyes frightened him. "Take your foot out of the door and I'll give you a hundred shillings, just so that we part friends. All right?"

"You can keep your hundred shillings," said the Piper, baring his sharp, pointed little teeth. "I'll find some other way for you and your town to pay for my services." And he turned and strode off.

When he had gone, the Mayor breathed a sigh of relief and then he dragged his oldest son out of bed. "Run round to the town clerk's house and tell him to organise a party at the town hall for midday. Wine and food for everyone in Hamelin."

"Can the children come too, Daddy?"

"Certainly not. Do you think the town is made of money? The children will have to stay at home *and behave themselves*. Now hurry."

What a party it was! They drank toast after toast to the Mayor. After looking round to see that the tall, sinister stranger had not come, he climbed on to a table and gave a speech. "Finally and in conclusion," he said, "I sent the foreigner away with not so much as a brass penny. In short, I saved you from the rats free of charge!"

But the children heard it.

First one child ran into the square and stood staring at the Piper. Then another flashed past, turning somersaults. Then another, and another. Some danced, some skipped, some leap-frogged, some hopscotched across the paving stones. Soon every child in Hamelin was playing in the square. The Pied Piper got to his feet and walked towards the city gates. And a sea of children followed after him. Some ran home and fetched their baby sisters and brothers to carry in the parade. They sang as they walked out of Hamelin towards the river. No-one got tired as they crossed the river by the bridge and climbed the slopes of the violet mountain.

That afternoon the grown-ups returned home from their celebration.

Slowly, one by one, the parents realised that their children were missing.

"The Mayor has five children. He must know where they've gone."

"That's it! Ask the Mayor! The Mayor has the answer to everything!"

They found the Mayor sitting on the

Outside in the town square the only grown-up in Hamelin not to be invited to the party sat by the fountain. The Pied Piper was polishing his flute again.

Soon he put the pipe to his lips and began to play. It was not the sad, haunting tune of the night before, but cheerful, dancing music. Such a lot of music from such a small pipe! It floated across the square and into every alley, it echoed in every doorway, it drifted over every rooftop. They did not hear it at the town hall, of course, the music at the party was so loud that it drowned the Piper's tune.

steps of his house, weeping for the loss of his five children. "If only I had kept my promise!" he was saying over and over again. "If only I had kept my word!" Clutched in his hand was the note he had found pinned to his door. It read: *For the removal of one million rats: 253 children of Hamelin. Payment received.* It was signed, 'The Pied Piper'.

As the Mayor handed over his chain of office to the unhappy townspeople, the notes of a pipe could just be heard from the slopes of the violet mountain beyond the river. But the children of Hamelin were never seen again.

Thumbelina

There once was a wife who longed for a little child. After many years of waiting, she had almost given up hope, but she went to a wise old woman and said, "Please can you help me? I would so love to have a little child."

"That shouldn't be too difficult," replied the old woman. "Just take this grain of corn, plant it by your front door and watch what happens."

So the wife went home and planted the grain of corn. In the warm spring sunshine, it quickly took root and grew — but the plant that sprang up from the soil was not corn. It was a magnificent flower with a single bud of red and yellow petals. The wife was so thrilled at the sight that she cupped her hands around the bud and kissed it.

At once the flower opened and there in the centre sat a tiny child — not a baby, but a perfectly formed young girl. She was beautiful and delicate, and exactly the size of the woman's thumb.

"I shall call you Thumbelina," said the woman, delighted at her good fortune. She made a cradle for the flower child out of half a walnut shell, with a rose-petal for a bed cover. And for several months, they lived together happily in the country cottage. While the woman worked in the kitchen or tended the garden, Thumbelina would perch nearby and sing or tell stories to make the hours pass quickly.

But their joy was not to last. One night as Thumbelina lay asleep in her tiny bed, a big, ugly toad hopped into the room through an open window, and peered at the sleeping girl. "What a beauty! She would make a lovely wife for my son," croaked the toad. And she picked up the walnut shell, sprang back out through the window, and hopped off to her home in the muddiest part of the river-bank.

"Look what I've got for you," she called to her son. "Don't you think she's pretty?" The son — who was almost as ugly as his mother — goggled at Thumbelina and just croaked in amazement.

"Be quiet or you'll wake her," snapped his mother. "Now you start making a home for her, while I make sure she can't escape." Then the fat old toad swam out to the farthest water-lily leaf and left Thumbelina there, still fast asleep.

When the tiny girl woke next morning — to find herself stranded on a leaf in the middle of a stream — she was terrified. Then the toad and her son came swimming out to see her. "This is to be your husband," said the fat old toad. "We are decorating a house in the mud for you

to live in." And off they swam again, leaving Thumbelina stranded on the lily.

Thumbelina burst into tears. She did not want to marry the ugly toad and live in a house of mud. But help was already at hand. The little fishes of the stream had heard what the old toad had said, and as soon as she had gone they popped their heads out of the water to look at the tiny girl.

"Please save me from the toads," she pleaded, tears rolling down her cheeks. "I don't want to be married." So the little fishes nibbled through the stem that anchored the lily leaf, and it floated away down the stream.

Thumbelina was happy to have escaped that she sang out loud for joy. Then a butterfly, hearing her voice, landed on the leaf. Thumbelina took a silk ribbon from her dress and tied one end to the butterfly's waist and the other to the leaf. Away the butterfly flew again, and soon they were racing along together down the stream.

But a big, ratty beetle with leathery wings had also heard Thumbelina singing. He swooped down to take a closer look, and was so struck by the flower-child's beauty that he grabbed her in his claws and carried her to a high tree. Thumbelina was quaking with fear,

but did not dare struggle in case she fell.

The beetle set her down on the topmost leaf and gave her honey to eat. He told her how lovely she was — even though she did not look like a beetle — and at first he wanted to marry her. But when his lady friends came visiting, they did not encourage him. "She has only two legs and looks just like a human being! How ugly!"

The beetle was soon convinced that Tumbelina really *was* ugly, so he carried her down to the foot of the tree and placed her on a daisy. She could go home, for all he cared.

But where could Thumbelina go? She had no home to go to. So she stayed where the beetle had left her. She wove a hammock of grass and hung it under a dock leaf for shelter. She ate honey from the flowers and drank the dew on their leaves each morning. And all summer long she lived there at the foot of the beetle's tree.

Then autumn came, and winter. The flowers withered and so did Thumbelina's flower-petal clothes. She could find neither food nor shelter. It began to snow and she was afraid she might freeze to death.

Wrapped in a shrivelled leaf, Thumbelina picked her way through a field of stubble, looking for grains of corn. At last she came to a hole in the ground where a field-mouse lived. She stood shivering outside the door and begged, "Please help me — I'm so cold, and I've nothing at all to eat."

"You poor little thing," said the field-mouse. "Come into my warm house and dine with me." The field-mouse had no children of her own, and she was lonely. "You can stay here for the winter if you will keep my house tidy and tell me a story every day."

Thumbelina was happy living with the field-mouse. It was like being back in the old wife's cottage — she felt safe again. But one day the field-mouse's friend, and elderly mole, came to visit. The field-mouse told Thumbelina that the mole was very rich — he had a wonderful black fur coat and his house was twenty times bigger than the field-mouse's.

"You must sing to him as sweetly as you can," she said, "and tell him all your best stories. If only he would marry you, you would always be well provided for."

Poor Thumbelina had not the slightest wish to marry the mole, but because the field-mouse had been so kind to her, she sang and entertained the mole as charmingly as she could. He was enchanted with her lovely singing voice, and the following week he invited Thumbelina and the field-mouse to supper.

The mole led them down the long, dark underground passage to his home. On the way down they tripped over something cold and feathery. The mole opened an overhead skylight to see what it was. "Ha," he said. "It's nothing but a dead swallow. How unfortunate to be a bird! All they can do is chirp all summer — and when winter comes, they die of starvation." Then he kicked the bird aside with one of his short, blunt legs.

But Thumbelina felt sorry for the bird, and could not stop thinking about it — even when the mole started telling her jokes. On the way home that night, she put her head for an instant against the bird's breast, then jumped back in surprise. Very, very faintly, she could hear the swallow's heart ticking away!

After the field-mouse had gone to bed, Thumbelina tip-toed back down the passage. She wrapped the swallow in a blanket made of hay and held out some water on a leaf for him to drink.

At last the swallow spoke, "Thank you, my sweet child. I feel much better now. Soon I shall be strong enough to fly."

"No, no, it's cold outside — you would freeze. You must stay here."

So Thumbelina tended the sick swallow all through the winter. And all through the winter she told stories to the field-mouse and sang sweetly to the mole.

During the cold, dark months, Thumbelina dreamed of summer, and longed to be out in the open air again. But on the first day of spring, the field-mouse greeted her with some news. "You're a lucky girl, Thumbelina, the mole wants to marry you!"

Thumbelina burst into tears. "But I don't want to marry. The mole is so old! And if I married him I'd have to live underground with him for ever!"

"Fiddlesticks!" squeaked the field-mouse. "He'll make you an excellent husband. Any more nonsense and I'll bite you with my white teeth!"

The mole came visiting every day, and Thumbelina grew more and more desperate. The wedding was less than a week away. Then late one night, when she tip-toed off to nurse the swallow, she found him stretching and flexing his wings. "At last I feel strong enough to fly, Thumbelina! You have saved my life. Is there anything I can do to thank you?"

"Oh, please take me with you!" cried Thumbelina, scarcely daring to hope. "Help me escape from the mole!"

"Climb onto my back then, and we will fly far away from here."

As the dawn broke, they opened the skylight in the passage and flew out into the rising sun. Up and away they soared, further and further, until they reached a warm land where it was already summer. At last they landed in a field of brilliant flowers. There the swallow set Thumbelina down beside a beautiful, red and yellow bud.

"What a lovely creature!" said a young man's voice. "Do stay here with us."

Thumbelina looked up in astonishment to see a handsome prince, no bigger than herself, standing in the flower. Bowing deeply, the prince took of his golden crown and placed it on her head, then asked Thumbelina, "Will you stay and be our Queen of the Flowers?"

She hesitated . . . then fairies came from each flower in the field, bearing her gifts. One — the smallest and sweetest of all the fairies — brought a pair of wings, so that Thumbelina could fly as they did. Then the prince asked again, "*Will* you stay here? And be my bride?"

Thumbelina answered, "Yes, of course." And the swallow sang for them as sweetly as he knew how, the whole summer long.

JACK AND THE BEANSTALK

Once upon a time, there was a poor widow who had an only son called Jack. Jack was not much help to his mother. He did not earn any money, and the two of them were very, very poor. Then, one day, their one cow finally became too old to give any more milk.

"It's no use," said Jack's mother. "We'll just have to sell her."

So Jack led the cow off towards the market, promising to get the best possible price for her. But the journey was long and boring, and Jack passed the time dreaming about what he would buy if he were rich.

On his way he met a funny little man with a big head and a tiny body, who offered to buy the cow.

"Give her to me and I promise you'll be rich to the end of your days," he said, holding out a small drawstring bag.

Jack could hardly believe his ears. But when he opened the bag instead of gold coins, he found it contained only five shrivelled beans!

"Those beans are magic," said the little man. "Plant them and they'll grow right up to the sky!" And before Jack could say anything he vanished — and so did the cow!

Jack ran home, wondering what would happen when he planted his magic beans.

"You were quick," said his mother, when Jack arrived home. "How much did you get for the cow?"

"I struck a wonderful bargain," he said. "Look at this!"

When his mother looked inside the bag she was furious. "Beans! Beans? You stupid, lazy good-for-nothing boy! Do you want us to starve?"

Jack tried to tell her that the beans were magic, but she would not listen. She flung them out through the window, then beat poor Jack and packed him off to bed without any supper.

The next morning, a very hungry Jack woke early. At least he *thought* it must be early because the room was so dark. But when he turned over he saw a huge green plant outside the window with giant leaves pushing through the shutters. "So! The beans were magic ones after all!"

Quick as a flash, Jack clambered out through the window and on to the enormous beanstalk. Stopping only to wave goodbye to his astonished mother standing below him, Jack began to scale the giant plant.

He climbed and climbed. He even climbed right through the clouds.

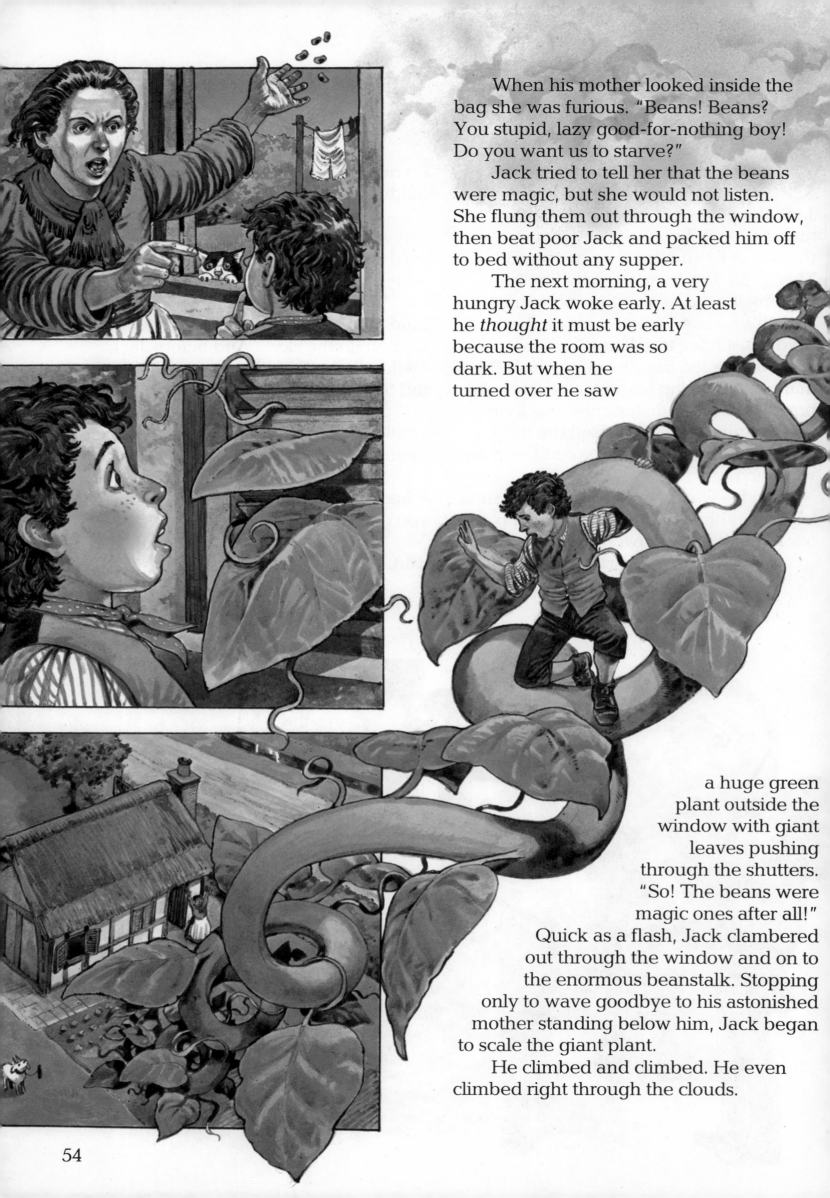

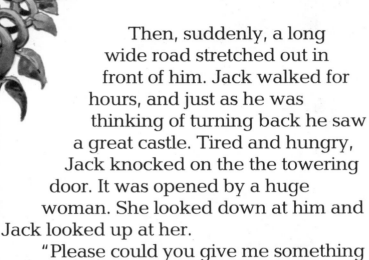

Then, suddenly, a long wide road stretched out in front of him. Jack walked for hours, and just as he was thinking of turning back he saw a great castle. Tired and hungry, Jack knocked on the the towering door. It was opened by a huge woman. She looked down at him and Jack looked up at her.

"Please could you give me something to eat?" he asked. "I'm very hungry."

"Be off with you. My husband will be back soon and he eats little boys like you for dinner."

But Jack pleaded with her, and in the end she let him in and gave him some bread and cheese. He had almost finished, when he heard great footsteps thudding along the passage.

"Oh dear!" cried the giant's wife. "It's my husband. Quick, hide in the oven."

Jack just had time to scramble into the oven when the kitchen door flew open and a great big bald-headed giant burst in. He sniffed in the air and roared:

Fee, fi, fo, fum,
I smell the blood of an Englishman.
Be he alive or be he dead,
I'll grind his bones to make my bread.

"No, no, no, dear," said his wife calmly. "You're mistaken. Now sit down and eat youre meal."

When the giant had finished his colossal dinner he took out a vast box full of bags and sat down to count his money. Peeping out from the oven, Jack caught his breath at the sight of so much gold!

Soon, the giant's head began to nod and he dropped off to sleep. Jack leaped out, threw one of the bags over his shoulder and sprinted out of the castle. He ran all the way along the road, then dropped the bag down on to the ground far below and clambered through the greenery of the beanstalk to his house.

For months Jack and his mother lived very well, but soon only a few gold coins remained. And one day, when his mother went to wake him, she found he had gone back up the beanstalk to find more gold.

"Oh, it's you again, is it?" said the giant's wife when she opened the castle door. "The last time you where here my husband lost a bag of gold."

"Really?" replied Jack. "How strange! Perhaps I can help you look for it. I'm small enough to fit in all the nooks and crannies you giants can't reach."

So the foolish giant's wife let Jack into the house again, and she even gave him some bread and cheese.

Jack was still pretending to look for the lost gold when he heard the footsteps of the giant coming home. He just had time to dive into the oven when the door burst open and the giant sniffed the air and roared:

Fee, fi, fo, fum,
I smell the blood of an Englishman.
Be he alive or be he dead,
I'll grind his bones to make my bread!

"No, no, no, my dear. I think you're mistaken. There's no-one here. Now sit down and eat your meal."

The giant held a little white hen in his hand, and when he had finished his meal he put it on the table. "Hen, hen, one two three, lay a golden egg for me!" and the hen laid the strangest egg Jack had ever

seen. It was made of solid gold! The giant chuckled greedily and then nodded off to sleep, clutching the golden egg.

Jack sneaked out of the oven, clamped his hand round the hen's neck and sprinted out of the castle, along the road and back down the beanstalk.

With the magic hen strutting around their yard, Jack and his mother were rich at last, and they said they would be happy for ever. But one morning, when his mother went to wake him, Jack had gone!

This time when Jack climbed the beanstalk and reached the castle door, he did not dare to knock, but crept inside while the giant's wife was fetching in the washing. And instead of hiding in the oven, he hid in the washtub.

Soon, he heard the footsteps of the giant in the passage and the door burst open. The giant sniffed the air and roared:

Fee, fi, fo, fum,
I smell the blood of an Englishman.
Be he alive or be he dead,
I'll grind his bones to make my bread!

"Surely not," said his wife. "But if you *can* smell that thieving boy who stole your bag of gold and your hen, he'll be hiding in the oven for sure."

The giant pounced on the oven door — but of course Jack was not inside.

"You really shouldn't upset yourself like that," said the giant's wife. "Now, why don't you get out your little harp?"

So the giant did. "Play," he said. And the little harp began to play sweet music.

The giant sighed happily, his wife sighed happily — and they both dozed off to sleep in their chairs.

Quick as a flash Jack jumped out of the washtub, snatched up the harp and ran out of the door. Then, suddenly, the harp cried out, "Master! Master! I'm being stolen!"

The giant woke up with a start. "What! Hey you! Stop! Bring me my axe!" Jack sprinted down the long road, the giant gaining with every stride, his massive feet pounding and his huge voice roaring for Jack's blood.

Jack reached the beanstalk just a few paces ahead of the giant, threw himself into its green mass, and slithered down the trunk. The bellowing giant tumbled after him, crashing through the branches, swinging his axe wildly.

"Fetch my axe!" Jack shouted to his mother as he reached the ground. Working furiously, Jack chopped away at the stem of the beanstalk as the giant emerged through the clouds. Then, with a creak and a groan, the beanstalk began to fall. It fell right through the roof, through the house — CRASH! — on to the ground. And the giant fell headlong into the vegetable patch with a mighty roar, and broke his neck!

Then Jack showed his mother the harp and asked it to play sweet music.

With the hen that laid golden eggs, and the harp that made such lovely music, Jack and his mother lived happily for the rest of their days.

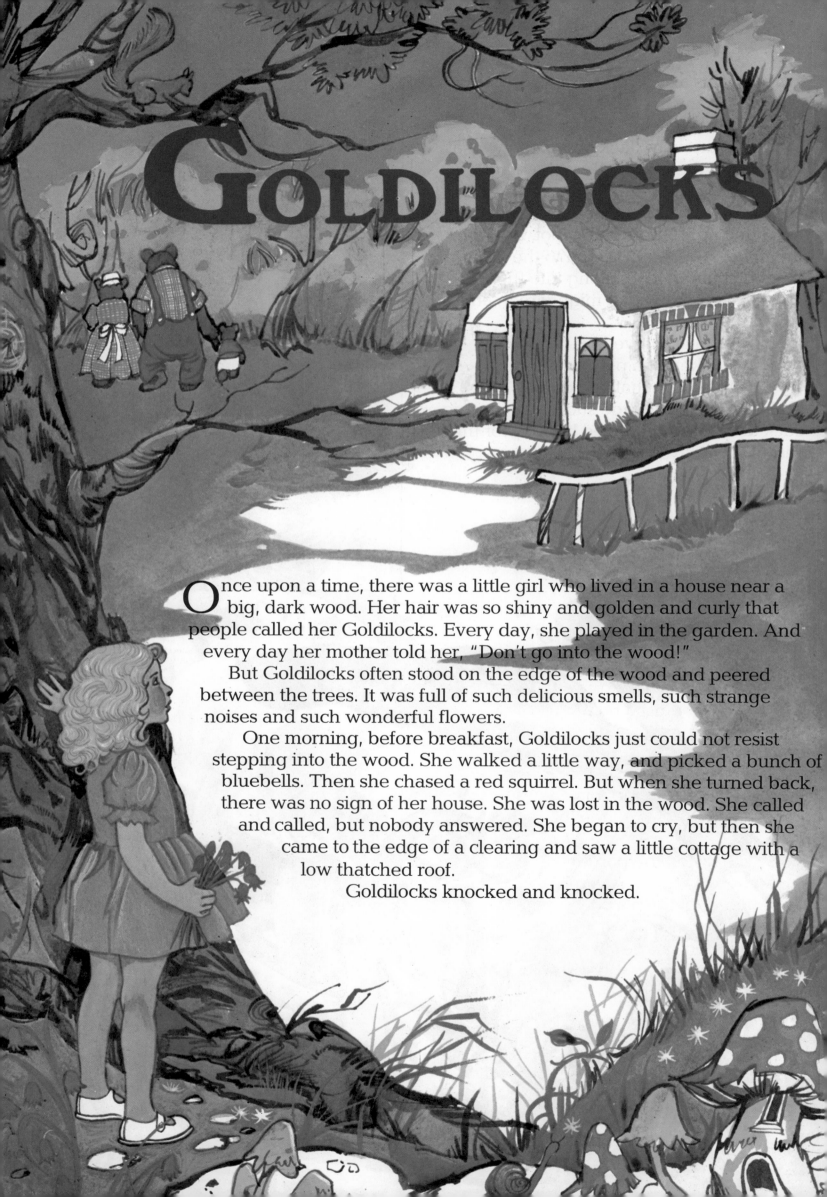

GOLDILOCKS

Once upon a time, there was a little girl who lived in a house near a big, dark wood. Her hair was so shiny and golden and curly that people called her Goldilocks. Every day, she played in the garden. And every day her mother told her, "Don't go into the wood!"

But Goldilocks often stood on the edge of the wood and peered between the trees. It was full of such delicious smells, such strange noises and such wonderful flowers.

One morning, before breakfast, Goldilocks just could not resist stepping into the wood. She walked a little way, and picked a bunch of bluebells. Then she chased a red squirrel. But when she turned back, there was no sign of her house. She was lost in the wood. She called and called, but nobody answered. She began to cry, but then she came to the edge of a clearing and saw a little cottage with a low thatched roof.

Goldilocks knocked and knocked.

me to sit in these chairs." So she sat in the biggest chair. But though she wriggled and squirmed, she could not get comfortable. "This chair's much too big." So she tried the middle-sized chair. "This chair's much too hard." Then she tried the smallest chair. But when Goldilocks sat down, the little chair gave way and broke into tiny pieces!

Picking herself up, Goldilocks went upstairs. In the bedroom, she found three beds — a big one, a middle-sized one and a small one.

"Oh, I'm so sleepy, and there's nobody here but me to lie on these beds."

Nobody answered . . . but the door suddenly swung open. Inside she saw a big wooden table, and on it three bowls of porridge — a big one, a middle-sized one and a small one.

"Oh, I'm so hungry," thought Goldilocks creeping indoors, "and there's nobody here but me to eat this porridge."

So she tasted the porridge in the biggest bowl. "Ow! That's much too hot." She tasted the porridge in the middle-sized bowl. "Ooh, that's far too cold." Then she tasted the porridge in the smallest bowl — it was just right. In fact, it tasted so good that she ate it all up!

Looking round, she saw three chairs — a big one, a middle-sized one and a small one. "Oh, I'm so tired, and there's nobody here but

So she lay down on the biggest bed where she tossed and turned for a while. "No, no. This bed is much too hard." Then she lay on the middle-sized bed and almost sank out of sight. "This bed is much too soft!" So she lay on the smallest bed — and that was just right. In fact it was so comfortable that she soon fell fast asleep.

Meanwhile, the family who lived in the cottage came back from walking in the wood: Father Bear, Mother Bear and Baby Bear!

"Our porridge will be cool enough to eat by now," said Father Bear.

"I do hope so, my dear," said Mother Bear.

"And so do I," said Baby Bear. "I'm very hungry."

But as soon as they opened the cottage door, they saw that something was wrong. Their three spoons had all been dipped into the breakfast bowls!

"*Who's been eating my porridge!*" roared Father Bear.

"*And who's been eating my porridge!*" exclaimed Mother Bear.

"*And who's been eating my porridge,*" squealed Baby Bear, "*and eaten it all up!*"

"*Never mind,*" said Mother Bear. "Daddy will give you some of his. Let's sit down and eat."

That was when they noticed the chairs. "*Who's been sitting in my chair!*" roared Father Bear.

"*And who's been sitting in my chair!*" exclaimed Mother Bear.

"*And who's been sitting in my chair,*" squealed Baby Bear, "*and broken it all to pieces!*"

So the three Bears began to prowl around the house, looking for the thief who had eaten Baby Bear's porridge and broken his chair. Slowly they climbed the

stairs. Father Bear went first. Mother Bear went second. And Baby Bear went third. With his huge paw, Father bear opened the bedroom door.

"*Who's been sleeping in my bed!*" he roared.

"*And who's been sleeping in my bed!*" exclaimed Mother Bear.

"*And who's been sleeping in my bed,*" squealed Baby Bear. "*and she's still there!*"

At that very moment, Goldilocks woke to see three bears leaning over her — a little one, a middle-sized one and a big one. She gave a scream and leaped off the bed, out of the window and did not stop running until she came to the edge of the wood.

There stood her own little home, and her mother on the kitchen step anxiously calling her name.

"Oh Mother! Mother! It was awful! It was terrible! It was dreadful!" sobbed Goldilocks, and she told her the story of the three bears.

Her mother dried her tears and gave Goldilocks a breakfast of bread and honey. But she said rather sternly, "Every day I tell you not to go into the wood. And now you know why."

"I promise I'll never go there again," said Goldilocks. "Never, never, never!" Then she ate three slices of bread and honey — a little one, a middle-sized one and a big one.

Feb 23, 91

Feb 23, 91